Inside the box were clothes, uniforms, shoes and hats …
an outfit for every job you could think of. *Which one
will the box choose for me today?* she wondered, her
eyes sparkling.

The tingling spread up her arms. Tara closed her eyes.
The attic was spinning away and she found herself tumbling
through space and time.

She was going on another adventure!

Chapter 2

When Tara opened her eyes, she was standing in an Accident and Emergency department in a hospital. It was very busy. A nurse was putting a bandage around a girl's knee and there was a boy with a bandage on his head.

Tara looked down at herself. She was wearing a white coat and blue cotton scrub trousers. She had a stethoscope around her neck. There was a watch clipped to her top pocket.

Tara Binns
Double-quick Doctor

Written by Lisa Rajan
Illustrated by Alessia Trunfio

Collins

Chapter 1

Tara Binns was in the attic at the top of her house. She was looking for the old costume box. It was her favourite thing in the whole house.

There it was!

Tara pushed open the heavy lid. Her fingers tingled, as they always did when she opened the box. Something special was about to happen.

"Hi, Doctor Binns," said a girl dressed in exactly the same way. "I'm Ayesha, the doctor in charge. It's going to be busy today – we've already got all kinds of accidents and emergencies!"

"I'm a doctor!" said Tara. "But I don't know how to cure illnesses or save lives. I wouldn't know where to start!"

"Don't worry," smiled Ayesha. "Watch me! Doctors have years of training," she told Tara. "But every patient is different, and you have to work out what to do each time. So you *Stop*, *Look* and *Listen*.

"First you *Stop* and check a patient's vital signs. Are they breathing? Is their heart beating too fast or too slow?"

She held two fingers inside Tara's wrist to check her pulse.

"Next, you *Look* for signs – a rash, bleeding, swelling – "
Ayesha checked Tara's arms.

"Then you *Listen* to their symptoms. Are they in pain?
Feeling dizzy? Hot or cold?" She put her hand on
Tara's forehead.

"And then you put it all together – "

BEEP! BEEP! BEEP!

Ayesha's bleep was going off.

"An ambulance!" she said. "Come on, Doctor Binns!"

Chapter 3

Ayesha hurried outside. An ambulance had just arrived, with lights flashing.

"A boy has been hit by a car!" called one of the paramedics, as she swung the back doors open.

Tara looked inside. A boy in a red and blue football kit was lying on a stretcher. He looked pale and very glum. He was holding his left arm.

A girl was sitting beside him. She was holding a sports bag and she looked very worried.

Paramedics lowered the stretcher out of the ambulance. They wheeled it through the hospital doors. Ayesha jogged alongside it.

"What happened?" Tara asked the girl, as the two of them followed behind.

"I'm Molly. That's my brother Ollie. We were playing in a football tournament and Ollie scored a hat-trick in his semi-final! There was a talent scout watching and he asked Ollie to try out for the Youth Academy.

"Ollie was so excited, he ran across the road to tell me. He didn't look and he got hit by a car."

Ayesha checked Ollie over.

"You were very lucky – you've had a nasty shock but you're OK …" Ayesha told Ollie, "… apart from your arm. It looks broken. Doctor Binns, could you take Ollie to Ortez for an X-ray, please? And tell his sister to wait for him in the waiting room."

BEEP! BEEP! BEEP!

Ayesha's bleep went off again.

"Next emergency – a boy with a jelly bean stuck up his nose!"

Chapter 4

Ortez was waiting for them inside the X-ray room.

"Come and sit down," said Ortez. "Rest your left arm on the table … palm facing up. Oh! You'll need to take that medical wristband off. It will block the X-rays."

Ollie slipped it off and handed it to Tara.

"What's it for?" she asked.

"A peanut allergy," replied Ollie. "I have to carry a special injector pen with me all the time. My mum's the same – she nearly died once. The wristband lets people know about it – in case I have an allergic reaction and can't speak."

Ortez put the X-ray machine over Ollie's arm.

"That's it. Now … keep your arm really still." Ortez and Tara stood away from the X-ray.

CLICK!

Ortez took X-ray pictures of …

CLICK!

… Ollie's arm …

CLICK!

… in three different positions.

Ortez looked at the pictures on the screen.

"Well?" asked Ollie with dread in his voice. "Is it broken?"

"I'm afraid so," said Ortez, gently. "We'll need to put your arm in a cast, to keep it still while the bone heals."

"How long for? The talent scout said the trials are next week. I can't miss them!" wailed Ollie.

"Six weeks," said Ortez. "I'm sorry. You'll have to stop playing football in case you fall over or knock your arm."

"But this was my big chance!" Tears filled Ollie's eyes.

Tara felt very sorry for him.

"Look," she said, kindly, "maybe the Youth Academy can put off your trial for a couple of months."

"Would they do that?" sniffed Ollie, wiping his eyes.

"It's worth asking – " Tara suggested. "I'll go and tell your sister what's happening."

Tara headed back to the waiting room.

Chapter 5

Tara spotted Molly sitting with a girl holding a bag of pick 'n' mix sweets.

Oh no! Something was wrong. Very wrong. Molly was clutching her throat. She was struggling to breathe. Tara ran over to her. Too late! Molly collapsed on to the floor, knocking the bag of sweets out of the girl's hand.

Tara looked around urgently for a doctor. She couldn't see anyone.

"Ayesha!" she shouted.

Tara's heart started pounding in her chest. She dropped to her knees beside Molly's limp body. What should she do?

Ayesha's voice echoed in her head ... *Stop, Look* and *Listen* ...

She grabbed Molly's wrist. Her pulse was racing.

Tara checked Molly's breathing. It was raspy and shallow ... and getting weaker. There was something dripping down the side of Molly's mouth. Was it blood? No ... it looked like ... smelt like ... chocolate.

What should she do? Where *was* Ayesha?

"What happened?" she asked the other girl.

"I don't know!" said the girl. "We were chatting about how we've both ended up spending the afternoon in a hospital because of our brothers. Mine was doing tricks with a jelly bean. Hers ran in front of a car. So I shared my sweets to cheer us both up. Then she started coughing and wheezing. Then she passed out."

Tara's brain began whirring. *Stop, Look and Listen … then put it all together …*

Ollie's medical wristband …

His mum nearly died …

Molly was struggling to breathe …

People in the same family can have the same allergy …

The chocolate by her mouth …

Tara's gaze fell on the pick 'n' mix sweets. Were some of them chocolate-covered peanuts?

She took one and popped it in her mouth. YES!

Ollie was allergic to peanuts. So maybe Molly was allergic too? Perhaps she took a chocolate from the pick 'n' mix bag without realising there was a peanut inside it. Tara pushed back Molly's sleeve. There it was – a medical wristband, just like Ollie's!

Molly was having a severe allergic reaction. If Tara didn't stop it and help her breathe … RIGHT NOW… Molly was going to die.

Chapter 6

What could she do? Tara thought her own heart was going to stop. Wait a second … hadn't Ollie said he always carried a special injector pen with him?

Tara grabbed the kit bag. She ripped the zip open and started hunting for the pen.

"What happened?" came a voice over Tara's shoulder. It was Ayesha! *Thank goodness she's here*, thought Tara.

"I think she's having an allergic reaction to peanuts," spluttered Tara, pointing to Molly's wristband. "I think she ate one by mistake. She was coughing and wheezing … and then she collapsed."

"Help me get her on this stretcher, Doctor Binns," said Ayesha, looking serious. "If you're right, this is an emergency. She needs an injection urgently!"

Within seconds, Ayesha was pushing Molly into a cubicle.

Just as Ayesha was about to close the curtain behind her, she heard Tara shout her name.

"Ayesha! CATCH!"

Sailing through the air, straight into Ayesha's open hand, came the blue and orange injector pen.

Tara had found it in the kit bag. And not a moment too soon. Ayesha gave a quick thumbs-up before swishing the curtain closed.

Tara sat back on her heels and took a deep breath. A nurse rushed in and out of Molly's cubicle. She could hear machines beeping and Ayesha's voice firmly giving instructions. Then it all went quiet.

Tara tiptoed over to the cubicle and peeked around the curtain.

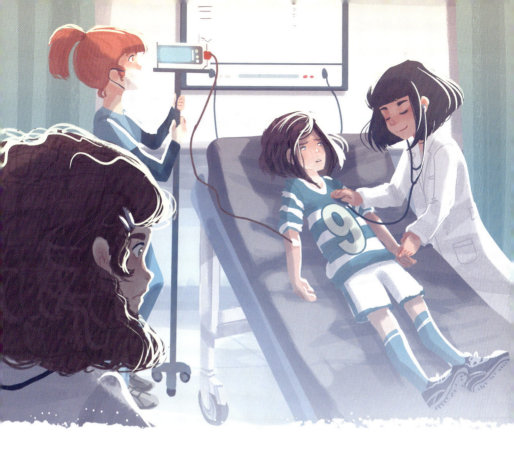

Ayesha was holding a stethoscope to Molly's chest. Tara watched as – slowly but surely – each rise and fall of Molly's chest was stronger than the last. The colour was returning to her cheeks. Her eyelids fluttered open.

Ayesha looked up and smiled at Tara.

"Well done, Doctor Binns! You were right. Your quick thinking saved Molly's life!"

Chapter 7

Sometime later, Molly was sitting up in a hospital bed.

"Thank you so much, Doctor Binns," she said, grinning broadly at Tara. "I would have died if it wasn't for you. You're amazing!"

"Thank you," smiled Tara. "But I just used my training – *Stop*, *Look* and *Listen*!"

Ollie sat beside her, his arm in a blue and red sling that matched his football kit. He looked very upset.

"Is your arm still hurting?" asked Tara.

"It's not that – " he sniffed.

"The football trials?" Tara suggested, gently.

"No … well, *yes* …" Ollie explained, "… but I feel bad that Molly nearly died and it was all my fault. If I had looked before crossing that road, we wouldn't have ended up in hospital. And Molly wouldn't have eaten that chocolate peanut – " he trailed off. "Thank goodness you worked out what was wrong, Doctor Binns."

"Well … you helped me," smiled Tara. "You told me about your wristband, the peanut allergy and your mum."

Molly gave Ollie a hug.

"Don't worry," she said, "I'm fine! But next time you cross a road … think of Doctor Binns and *Stop*, *Look* and *Listen*!"

Tara was very pleased that Ollie and Molly were going to be OK.

Ortez popped his head around the door.

"Good news, Ollie! The Football Academy just rang up to find out how you are. They'll postpone your trial for two months. Oh, and Molly – they want you to come at the same time! The talent scout was going to tell you but you jumped into the ambulance with Ollie!"

He turned to Tara. "Could you come with me? Ayesha and I need your help. We're taking out a jelly bean …"

"Does it need three of us?" Tara laughed.

"Teamwork, Doctor Binns!" said Ayesha. She held up her hand for a high five and the two of them clapped palms together.

At once, Tara's hand started tingling. The tingling spread up her arm. The hospital room started spinning … or was it her? Everything was whirling and swirling.

Chapter 8

The next moment, she was back home in her attic.

She took off the doctor's coat and put the stethoscope back in the costume box. What an adventure! She felt proud of herself. She liked working out what was wrong. She liked having to think quickly. And she loved helping to save lives – what an amazing feeling!

Tara closed the lid of the costume box.

Maybe I'll be a doctor when I grow up, she thought.
I'll find new ways to make my patients get better. I'll heal every patient I can. Heart-stopping decisions … breathtaking moments …

She grinned as she remembered the boy with the jelly bean.

Who 'nose' what accidents and emergencies will come my way?

Ayesha shows Tara how to *Stop, Look* and *Listen*

Stop

Look

Listen

Tara uses *Stop, Look* and *Listen*

Stop

Look

Listen

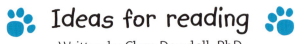

Ideas for reading

Written by Clare Dowdall, PhD
Lecturer and Primary Literacy Consultant

Reading objectives:
- ask questions to improve their understanding of a text
- draw inferences such as inferring characters' feelings, thoughts and motives from their actions, and justify inferences with evidence
- identify main ideas drawn from more than one paragraph and summarise ideas

Spoken language objectives:
- ask relevant questions to extend their understanding and knowledge

- give well-structured descriptions, explanations and narratives for different purposes
- use relevant strategies to build their vocabulary

Curriculum links: Science; PSHE – Health and wellbeing

Interest words: stethoscope, vital signs, symptoms, paramedics, injector pen, allergic reaction, cast

Resources: paper, pens and pencils

Build a context for reading

- Read the title and blurb together. Ask children to describe what they can see in the illustration.

- Challenge children to suggest what sort of doctor the picture is showing, and to share any experiences of accident and emergency (note that sensitivity may be needed here).

- Discuss what the phrase *Double-quick* means, drawing out the possible meanings for a doctor (e.g. having to react quickly in an emergency, having to make quick decisions).

Understand and apply reading strategies

- Ask for a volunteer to read pp2–5 aloud to the group. Praise and comment on fluent reading and the use of appropriate expression.

- Ask children to imagine how they would feel if they were in Tara's position at the hospital.